Down at Angel's

Down at Angel's

by **SHARON CHMIELARZ** *illustrated by* **JILL KASTNER**

TICKNOR & FIELDS BOOKS FOR YOUNG READERS · NEW YORK 1994

Published by Ticknor & Fields Books for Young Readers, A Houghton Mifflin company, 215 Park Avenue South, New York,
New York 10003. Text copyright © 1994 by Sharon Chmielarz. Illustrations copyright © 1994 by Jill Kastner. All rights reserved.
For information about permission to reproduce selections from this book, write to Permissions, Ticknor & Fields, 215 Park Avenue
South, New York, New York 10003. Manufactured in the United States of America. Book design by David Saylor.
The text of this book is set in 14 point New Baskerville Bold. The illustrations are oil paintings reproduced in full color.

HOR 10 9 8 7 6 5 4 3 2 1

Library of Congress Cataloging-in-Publication Data   Chmielarz, Sharon.   Down at Angel's / by Sharon Chmielarz ; illustrated by
Jill Kastner   p.   cm.   Summary: Though others think their neighbor Angel is a "dumb Bulgarian," a young girl and her little sister
enjoy watching him work and sharing a Christmas visit.   ISBN 0-395-65993-0   [1. Neighborliness—fiction. 2. Christmas—fiction.]
I. Kastner, Jill, ill. II. Title. PZ7.C4458Do 1994 [E]—dc20 93-11020 CIP AC

For Bev, Betty, and Marilyn

—S.C.

For Judy, Pasquale, and Louise

—J.K.

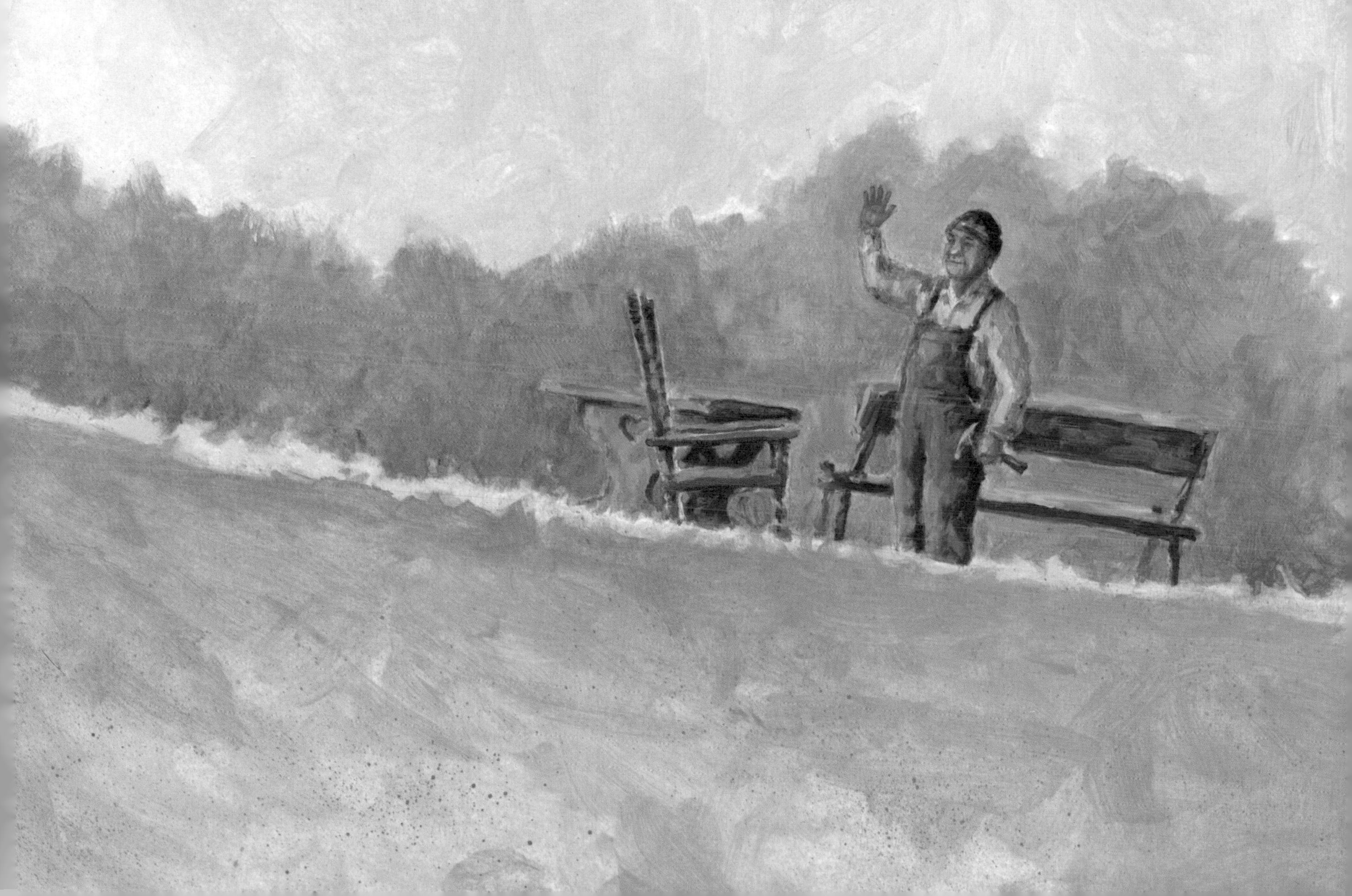

MY FRIEND ANGEL lives in his cellar. In the dim light from the window his tabletop shines like his supper—hard-boiled eggs and Spanish onions in a bowl.

"So, you want a bar of chocolate or a bite of garlic?" Angel always asks when my little sister and I visit him. Angel has one good eye, nut-brown and merry. The other eye is like a milky star and fools me.

"Do you help your mama now that your papa's passed on?" asks Angel.

I always nod, and the candy is ours.

Some kids like Angel. Others are afraid of his eye. The big kids next door call him "that dumb Bulgarian" and make fun of his accent.

Angel works in the railroad roundhouse. He throws the big lever that switches the tracks for trains.

But Angel was a woodworker in Bulgaria—an artist, Ma says. His cellar is full of wooden picture frames and puzzles, kitchen chairs and baby stools and cabinets.

Every Saturday, *whaannnng!* goes the buzz saw down at Angel's. Sawdust showers over his blue cap and shoulders, flies like a sandstorm across the saw table, and lies ankle-deep on the floor.

Whenever he turns the saw off, we can hear the radio playing. "Opera!" I yell. "We never listen to opera at home."

"We always listened at home in Sofia," Angel says.

Angel's house looks out over the tracks, across the valley to the hills along the Missouri River. Ma says his wife left him, and that's why his house is all run-down.

"Left him for heaven, like Dad in the war?" I ask, the only time I ever saved half a candy bar to eat at home.

"Left him to live in the East," Ma says.

"Why?" I ask.

"Don't step on the floor, I just waxed," she says. "And don't go bothering Angel for chocolate. Times are too hard for such extras."

In the spring, my little sister and I chop rhubarb stalks for Ma and make rhubarb-leaf hats for us. In the summer, we pick tomatoes and cucumbers for Ma to can. In the fall, we gather chokecherries and apples, and rake the yard, but afterward we always drop by Angel's to chew the fat and have a candy bar. When I remember Ma's words, the chocolate tastes even sweeter.

One fall day Angel shows us the upstairs of his house. "Watch the steps," he says, and leads the way.

"Look at all those plants!" I say. "Let's play jungle."

"Look at all the little buds on this one," my sister says.

"Look, but don't touch," Angel warns. "When the cactus blooms, it will be Christmas."

"Will Mrs. Angel come home then?" my sister asks.

When Angel doesn't answer, I walk over to the stack of tables Angel has for sale, tables with inlaid patterns—rings, houses, flowers, and, my favorite, the table with a star. "I'm going to buy this table when I grow up," I promise Angel.

"Where've you been?" Ma asks as usual when we come home.

"Down at Angel's," I say. "Ma, why did Angel's wife go away?"

"Everybody in town knows that."

"I don't."

"Well, he built that house for her, but he drank too much," Ma says slowly.

"Does he drink anymore?"

"No," she says. "Now he spends his drinking money on wood."

"No," I repeat. I tap-dance on the shiny blue floor she's just cleaned. "No, no more. 'Cause Angel's an angel. From Sofia, in Bulgaria. He lives in his cellar and has a sad star in one eye."

As late as the first snowfall, my sister and I sun like cats on stacks of lumber in Angel's yard, eating chocolate. "Christmas is coming," I say. "Maybe we should buy Angel a present." I stop munching. The chocolate doesn't taste so sweet anymore. We have no money! And I can't tell Ma about all the candy bars.

"Why so gloomy, girls?" Ma asks at four o'clock on Christmas Eve. She is happy. The baking is done, and the house is clean and ready. Any other day, we would go down to Angel's. But not today.

"We don't have anything to give Angel," I say.

My little sister pats her pockets. "No presents."

"Sure you do," Ma says. "How about something you've made? Angel would like that."

Ma pitches right in. She helps us take everything we need from our fruit closet. Then, when we have packed up a grocery box, Ma says she is coming, too. Coming down to Angel's!

Out through the back gate, down the alley, onto the snow-packed road. The box jiggles on the sled.

"All aboard!" I call.

"Giddyup!" my sister yells.

"The going's slick!" Ma shouts, laughing, trying to keep up with us.

Down to Angel's. Down the road. Down to the run-down house on the corner. What a caboose! What a ride! What a night!

Angel looks surprised to see Ma but takes the box
and sets it on the saw table under the light bulb. The
wrapping paper is speckled with silver and blue and
gold and green, and shines like a Christmas tree.

"Open it up!" we demand.

"First?" Angel asks. "What about the bar of chocolate?
What about the garlic?"

We look at Ma, who nods. She knows!

While we eat our candy bar, Angel admires our summer work: shining jars of rhubarb sauce, dill pickles, tomatoes, chokecherry jelly, apple butter.

"Try Ma's fruitcake!" I say.

Ma waves a hand to quiet me.

"Or a cookie," my little sister says.

"A popcorn ball," I say. "Or fudge—it cooled on our back porch!"

Angel takes a bite of this, a bite of that. "Just like in Sofia," he says. His eyes are closed. His smile is wide.

Ma looks around the cellar while her hand keeps time to the opera. No buzz saw interrupts the music tonight.

"Ready to go, girls?" she asks after we have eaten our chocolate.

"Not so fast," Angel says.

He goes upstairs. The floorboards creak over our heads as he walks across the living room. When he comes down he is carrying the table with the star.

"Oh, Angel!" I say.

"Not yet, not yet," he says, dusting off the tabletop with a swipe of one blue sleeve. On the underside he draws a capital *A* over a rose with a curving stem. "For you girls and your ma," Angel says.

"Thank you, Angel," we call, as the sled glides onto the road.

"Thank you," he answers, with the wink of a star.

We go home through the dark, warmed by the soft light from the cellar down at Angel's.